WITHDRAWN

Whose Hat Is That? by Peter Trumbull and Lori Reiser

©1995 Fisher-Price, Inc. ©1995 School Zone® Publishing Company
Fisher Price trademarks are used under license from Fisher-Price, Inc.
Manufactured for and distributed by: School Zone® Publishing Company
1819 Industrial Drive, P.O. Box 777, Grand Haven, MI 49417

ISBN 0-88743-437-1

The NASA logo is a trademark of the National Aeronautics and
Space Administration and is used with permission.

Whose Hat Is That?

Written by Peter Trumbull and Lori Reiser

Illustrated by Lori Reiser

Who wears a shiny,
red leather hat
to put out our fires
or rescue a cat?

A firefighter

Who wears a hat
that is hard and strong
and helps keep him safe
all the day long?

A construction worker

Who wears a straw hat
to begin the day
of riding a tractor
to bring in the hay?

A farmer

Who wears a striped hat
that we can spy
while watching a train
as it speeds by?

A train conductor

Who wears a blue hat
so we can see
that our town is safe
for you and me?

STOP

A police officer

POLICE

Whose hat is needed
to cover her face
and help her breathe
while she's in space?

An astronaut

NASA

Off to the moon!
See you soon.